This book
belongs to

....

Other books by Mick Inkpen

ONE BEAR AT BEDTIME

THE BLUE BALLOON

THREADBEAR

KIPPER

KIPPER'S BIRTHDAY

KIPPER'S BOOK OF COLOURS

KIPPER'S BOOK OF COUNTING

KIPPER'S BOOK OF OPPOSITES

KIPPER'S BOOK OF WEATHER

PENGUIN SMALL

LULLABYHULLABALLOO!

WHERE, OH WHERE, IS KIPPER'S BEAR?

WIBBLY PIG CAN MAKE A TENT

WIBBLY PIG MAKES PICTURES

WIBBLY PIG OPENS HIS PRESENTS

WIBBLY PIG CAN DANCE

WIBBLY PIG LIKES BANANAS

WIBBLY PIG IS UPSET

NOTHING

BILLY'S BEETLE

British Library Cataloguing in Publication data

A catalogue record for this book is available
from the British Library

ISBN 0-340-580496

Text and illustrations copyright © Mick Inkpen 1992

The right of Mick Inkpen to be identified as the author
of this work has been asserted by him in accordance with
the Copyright, Designs and Patents Act 1988.

First published by Hodder Children's Books 1992
Paperback edition first published 1993
20 19 18

Published by Hodder Children's Books
a division of Hodder Headline plc
338 Euston Road, London NW1 3BH

Printed in China for Imago

Kipper's Toybox

Mick Inkpen

Hodder
Children's
Books

a division of Hodder Headline plc

Someone or something had been
nibbling a hole in Kipper's toybox.

'I hope my toys are safe,' said
Kipper. He emptied them out and
counted them.

'One, two, three, four, five,
six, SEVEN! That's wrong!' he said.
'There should only
be six!'

Kipper counted his toys again.
This time he lined them up to
make it easier.

'Big Owl one, Hippopotamus two,
Sock Thing three, Slipper four,
Rabbit five, Mr Snake six.

'That's better!' he said.

Kipper put his toys back in
the toybox. Then he counted them
one more time. Just to make sure.
    'One, two, three, four, five,
six, seven, EIGHT NOSES! That's
two too many noses!' said Kipper.

Kipper grabbed Big Owl and
threw him out of the toybox.
    'ONE!' he said crossly.
Out went Hippopotamus, 'TWO!'
Out went Rabbit, 'THREE!'
Out went Mr Snake, 'FOUR!'
Out went Slipper, 'FIVE!'
But where was six? Where was
Sock Thing?

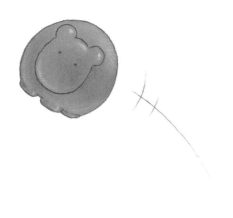

Kipper was upset. Next to Rabbit,
Sock Thing was his favourite.
Now he was gone.

'I won't lose any more of you,'
said Kipper. He picked up the rest of
his toys and put them in his basket.
Then he climbed in and kept watch
until bedtime.

That night Kipper was woken by a strange noise.

It was coming from the corner of the room.

Kipper turned on the light.
There, wriggling across the floor,
was Sock Thing! It must have
been Sock Thing who had been
eating his toybox!

Kipper was not sure what to do.
None of his toys had ever come to
life before. He jumped back in his
basket and hid behind Big Owl.

Sock Thing wriggled slowly round in a circle and bumped into the basket. Then he began to wriggle back the way he had come.

He did not seem to know where he was going. Kipper followed.

Quickly Kipper grabbed him
by the nose. Sock Thing squeaked
and wriggled harder.

Then a little tail appeared.
A little pink tail.

And a little voice said,
'Don't hurt him!'

'So it was YOU! You have been making the hole in my toybox!' said Kipper.

It was true. The mice had been nibbling pieces of Kipper's toybox to make their nest.

'You must promise not to nibble it again,' said Kipper.

'We promise,' said the mice.

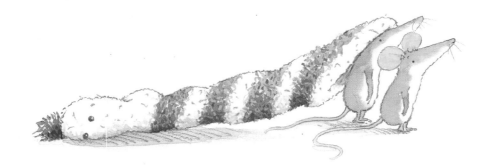

In return Kipper let the mice share his basket. It was much cosier than a nest made of cardboard and the two little mice never nibbled Kipper's toybox again...

But their babies did.
They nibbled EVERYTHING!